"ALWaYS
WeAr
CLeaN
UNdeRWeaR!"

"ALWAYS WEAR CLEAN UNDERWEAR!"

And Other Ways Parents Say "I Love You"

MARC GELLMAN

illustrated by
Debbie Tilley

HarperTrophy®
An Imprint of HarperCollinsPublishers

Harper Trophy® is a registered trademark of HarperCollins Publishers Inc.

"Always Wear Clean Underwear!"
Text copyright © 1997 by Marc Gellman
Illustrations © 1997 by Debbie Tilley
For information address HarperCollins Children's Books, a division of
HarperCollins Publishers, 1350 Avenue of the Americas, New York, NY 10019.

Library of Congress Cataloging-in-Publication Data
Gellman, Marc.
    "Always wear clean underwear": and other ways parents say "I love you" / Marc Gellman;
illustrated by Debbie Tilley.
        p.   cm.
    Summary: Explains the little and big meanings of things parents tell their children, such as
"Eat your vegetables," "Look both ways before you cross the street," and "Don't talk with
your mouth full."
    ISBN 0-688-14492-6 — ISBN 0-688-17112-5 (pbk.)
    1. Parent and child—Juvenile literature.   2. Child rearing—Juvenile literature.
[1. Behavior.   2. Parent and child.]   I. Tilley, Debbie, illus.   II. Title.
HQ772.5.G45   1997   97-6885
306.874—dc21   CIP
                                                                            AC

❖
First Harper Trophy edition, 2000
Visit us on the World Wide Web!
www.harperchildrens.com

For Sol, Rosalie, Arthur, and Mary,

who learned The List From:

Leo, Sarah, Max, Dora, The Governor, Fanny, Louis, and Brona,

and who taught The List to:

Marc, Judy, Joanne, Larry, Michael, Nancy, and Betty,

who have already taught The List to:

Mara, Max, Joshua, Ashley, Jessica, Hannah, Gregory, Marci,

Isaac, Mia, and Aaron,

who will someday teach The List to their children.

Contents

The List

Shut up, my Father explained.
  —Ring Lardner

ABOUT THE LIST

I wrote this book because of my mom's horrible green-bean casserole. The way she made it, the green beans were gray and mixed up with some awful mushroom goop and then covered with some bad-tasting crunchy brown onion things. I really hated my mom's green-bean casserole. I even hated Tuesdays, because that was usually the day I had to eat it. Mom would say to me in her do-it-or-else voice, "Eat your vegetables!" and that was that. I had to eat it, or I had to sit at the table for the rest of the night and eat it cold. And the one thing worse than my mom's hot green-bean casserole was my mom's *cold* green-bean casserole.

I'm sure the same thing has happened to you. Maybe you don't have to eat goopy green-bean casserole. Maybe in your house the horrible vegetable is spinach or lima beans or squash with smelly cheese on top. Part of being a kid seems to be living with grown-ups who make you eat vegetables you hate. I remember lots of other things my mom and dad told me to do (or not to do) over and over again.

I remember "Take out the garbage," "Stand up straight," "Clean your plate," "Don't hit," "Share your toys," "Always say please and thank you," "Always wear clean underwear," and lots more.

The amazing thing about this list of things my parents told me over and over again is that all kids seem to have been told the same things by their parents. It's really spooky. There's a list out there in the world of all the things that all parents should tell all children all the time. Nobody ever sends The List to parents. They don't get it at the hospital when they bring you home. They don't read it in a book or see it on television or hear it on the radio, but every parent still knows The List. Your grandparents heard The List and the children of your children will hear The List. The List is forever!

The reason I wrote down The List is that I now understand it was the way my folks showed me that they loved me. It was the way they tried to help me grow up into a good and kind and decent person with good manners and good friends and, someday, a good family of my own.

What I figured out is that everything your parents nag you about has a little meaning and a big meaning. I know you don't understand yet what kind of big meaning there could possibly be in eating vegetables or wearing clean underwear, but—believe me—it's there. When you learn the big meanings you'll become a better person. To grow up, you just have to be fed and watered and kept out of the rain and cold, but to grow up good you have to be taught The List.

In each chapter, I take one thing on The List and try to explain to you its little and its big meaning. I did this so that you won't hate The List or hate your folks for nagging you all the time. I did this so you will see how hard and how important it is to learn to be good. I did this because someday you may have to explain The List to your own kids and you may need some help. I did this because your parents have lots of ways to show you that they love you, and The List is one of the biggest ways.

After I finished this book, I called my mom and thanked her for showing me that she loved me by making me eat her green-bean casserole. She was pleased but a little confused. She asked me if I wanted the recipe. I told her that, truthfully, I never really liked her green-bean casserole. She said, "If I had known you hated it, I would have made you my creamed broccoli instead." I didn't have the courage to tell her that the only thing worse than her green-bean casserole was her creamed broccoli!

Good luck with The List and God bless us all real good.

Always wear clean underwear

Why do your parents care about your underwear? Nobody sees your underwear, and yet parents always tell kids to wear clean underwear. What gives?

If you ever ask your parents this question, they will give you answer #1: "Dirty underwear is full of germs, and we don't want those germs jumping off your underwear and onto you."

If you tell your folks that you can wear underwear for a month before it gets *really* dirty, they will give you answer #2. This answer is so goofy that lots of kids just fall down laughing when they first hear it, but it's one of the most famous answers on The List:

"You should always wear clean underwear because *if* you ever get into an accident on the way to school or on the way home from school *and* an ambulance has to take you to the hospital *and* the doctors in the emergency room have to take your pants off, if they see that you're wearing dirty underwear *then* they'll think that we're bad parents because we don't wash your underwear."

I don't know how these answers got started. Like most things on The List, they seem to have been around forever. I never heard of people getting sick from wearing dirty underwear. Maybe you could get sick from wearing somebody else's dirty underwear, but I just don't think you could get that sick from wearing your own. And I never ever heard of doctors in any emergency room saying, "Well, we'd like to help this kid, but we just can't—he's wearing dirty underwear."

So, there must be some big deep reason hiding behind why your folks care so much about clean underwear. I think I figured it out. The big reason for wearing clean underwear is to teach you this:

What people don't see about you should be just as good as what people do see about you.

We all try to look good outside. The hard part is to look good inside.

If you pretend to be somebody's friend but say bad things about him or her to other people, then it's a lot like wearing dirty underwear. If you look at your own test when the teacher is looking at you but as soon as the teacher leaves the room look at your neighbor's test, then you're wearing dirty underwear. If you act nice to your brothers or sisters when your parents are around but hit them and make them miserable when your parents are gone, then you're wearing dirty underwear.

The hardest thing in life is to be the same way deep down as you are on top. If you're always pretending to be something you aren't, if you never say what you mean, if you never do what you say, then you'll be unhappy, and people will stay away from you because they don't want to have a friend who is clean only on the outside.

Of course, nobody's perfect. One of the differences between good people and bad people is that good people don't try to hide their bad parts. They admit their bad parts and try to make their bad parts smaller. They take their bad parts to the laundry so that when they go out into the world, their insides and their outsides will both be clean.

And you know what? Wearing clean underwear

isn't so bad after all. Once you get used to the feeling of being the same on the inside as you are on the outside, you won't want to lie about anything anymore. Once you get used to really being nice to people and not just *acting* nice to people, you'll get used to the feeling of having real friends. And once you get used to the feeling of soft clean underwear next to your skin, you won't want to go scrounging around under the bed looking for the cootie-coated underwear you wore last Tuesday!

DON'T PEE IN THE POOL

You don't need to know how everything works, but you do need to know how *you* work. After you eat a hot dog, drink a soda, and dive into a swimming pool, this is how you work: Your body sends a message to your brain. This is the message: PEE NOW!

Your body does not care if you are having a good time swimming. Your body does not care if the bathroom is a long way from the pool. Your body does not care if you will get the shivers running there. Your body only cares about one thing, and that one thing is pee! So you have to decide right then and right there, right in that pool, to climb out of the pool, dry off, and go to the bathroom to take care of the pee message from your body, or...you can just pee in the pool.

You remember your parents telling you over and over again, "Don't pee in the pool!" Maybe they said it this way: "Listen! People don't swim in our toilet, so don't pee in their pool!" However they said it, they said it. So there you are, standing in the pool trying to decide whether to listen to your body or your folks, and you don't have much time to decide.

What makes the decision so hard is that nobody is ever going to catch you peeing in the pool. When you pee in a pool, there is no alarm that goes off, no sign that goes up saying, "Pee alert! Somebody just peed in the pool!" There are no pee police looking for yellow water in the pool. Peeing in the pool is one of those disgusting things you know you can do without ever getting caught. If you rob a bank, you will probably get caught. If you steal an airplane, you will probably get caught. If you try to hide an elephant in your room, you will probably get caught. But if you pee in the pool, nobody is going to catch you, and this is the big meaning of "Don't pee in the pool": *Don't do bad stuff, even if there is no chance that you will get caught.*

Your life will be full of chances to pee in the pool. There will be lots of times when you will be able to do some little disgusting thing that nobody will catch you doing. You probably won't get caught if you stick gum under a chair, kick a cat, write your name on a wall, or call a ball out when it is really in, but all these things are bad, and you should not do them if you want to be a good person and...it has *nothing* to do with getting caught.

Getting caught is one way to learn how to do the right thing, but it's not the best way. The best way is for you to catch yourself. You shouldn't do bad things just because they're bad, not because you might get caught. And you should do good things just because they're good, not because somebody will reward you.

Anyway, there are not enough pee police to catch all the people peeing in all the pools. In fact, there are no pee police, so we need people to stop all that peeing in all those pools all by themselves. And we have to stop all the other little disgusting things we all do because we can get away with them. So the next time you have a soda and a hot dog with some chips and gummy bears, remember to head for the bathroom *before* you head for the pool. The world, and the pool, will be just a little bit better, and just a little bit less yellow, all because of you.

EAT YOUR VEGETABLES

No one knows why the stuff that's bad for you tastes so good and why the stuff that's good for you tastes like celery. God just created the world that way, and it makes things very hard for your folks around dinnertime. I bet your parents have never said this to you: "You better eat your chocolate ice cream with marshmallow sauce and whipped cream and nuts with the cherry on top, or there will be no television for you!" I bet you've never heard, "If you don't eat your pizza, you can't have any more broccoli." But I will bet anything that your folks have told you a zillion times, "Eat your vegetables!" You will probably get told to eat your vegetables until the day you move out of the house and get your own place. Then you can eat cold pizza for breakfast, chocolate for lunch, and things with names that end in *-itos* for dinner.

It's the great stuff in vegetables that explains why your folks think it's worth it to nag you to eat them. That's the little meaning of this thing on The List. Veggies don't have any fat or sugar or salt or red dye number 92. Veggies are full of stuff that helps keep cancer out of you. Veggies make you fast and strong and help you live a long and healthy life. But there is not one single vegetable I know about that tastes as

good as chocolate cake with cold milk. That's the fact, Jack! When your parents nag you about eating your vegetables, what they're really trying to do is teach you a big lesson: *What you want is not always what you need.* Eating veggies is what you need, even if eating veggies is not what you want.

As you grow up, you are going to have lots of other choices that are like the choice between celery and chocolate. You are going to have to choose between things you need but don't want and things you want but don't need. You may want to watch television, but you need to read books. You may want to play video games, but you need to play outside. You may want to gossip, but you need to mind your own business. You may want to do drugs, but you need to stay clean. You may want to buy, but you need to save. You may want to eat things that come in cellophane wrappers, but you need to eat your veggies!

Now, things are really not so bad. Don't think of life as just a plate of celery sticks. Vegetables can be delicious. Lots of really great people eat only vegetables. Choosing to eat vegetables and choosing the things you need can be healthy and fun. In fact, the best way to know you have grown up into a good person is that when you take a deep breath and look around you, you say, "Finally, what I want is what I need." Anyway, as the Rolling Stones once said, you can't always get what you want—but if you try real hard, you just might find that you can get what you need. Ohhh, yeahhhhhhh!!

TAKE OUT THE GARBAGE

Our only choice about garbage is choosing who is going to take it out. You can sort your garbage and recycle the stuff in it that can be used again, but you can't decide to make *no* garbage. All people make garbage, because living makes garbage. If you don't want your house to be smothered by a mountain of garbage, somebody has to take it out of your house and put it in a place where somebody else can shlep it away.

Taking out the garbage is part of the kid's job in lots of families. Actually, it makes sense. You don't buy the food or cook the food or call the Chinese restaurant to order the food, so it's fair for you to pitch in and take what's left of the food out to the street for the garbage collectors to pick up in the morning.

Most of the time, taking out the garbage is no big deal. But sometimes you're out there, dragging the garbage can to the curb, and the can tips over, or the bag breaks, and there you are, standing ankle deep in a stinking pile of chicken bones, sardine cans, piles of old spaghetti, and globs of that tuna-fish casserole you had for last night's dinner, which everybody dumped in the garbage when your mom wasn't looking. You're the one who has to do the dirty job of

getting the spilled garbage back into the can or the bag. On the days when the garbage spills, you need to remember the deep lesson taking out the garbage is supposed to teach you: *You have to learn how to do hard, dirty jobs.*

Not every important job is easy or clean. When the electrical wires break in a storm, somebody has to climb the pole in the rain or snow to fix them. When the sewer line breaks, somebody has to crawl down the smelly sewer hole to fix it. When the circus parade ends, somebody has to clean up after the elephants. And when you get the chicken bones back into the garbage can, somebody still has to empty them into a truck, and cart them away, and dump them on a pile of other garbage, and cover the whole thing with enough dirt so that the entire town doesn't smell.

Your parents also want you to learn that some of the jobs of being in a family are not fun. When you were a little baby and you started crying in the middle of the night and needed comforting, or when you threw up all over them in the car and they needed to clean up, or when you needed to have your diaper changed right away, your parents did all those dirty jobs because they love you. And one of the ways we show our love for one another is by taking out the garbage for the people we love.

There are lots of hard, dirty jobs you might never have to do in your life, and another reason your parents make you take out the garbage is so that you will learn to respect the men and women who have to do those jobs. Hard, dirty work is just as important as clean, easy work, maybe even more important. Also, when you finally do decide what you want to do with your life, and you first start out doing it, the chances are that your boss will probably give you the hardest and longest and dirtiest job to do. When bosses were just starting out, they had to do those jobs, and now they figure it's your turn.

The thing is that the garbage just has to be taken out, and sometimes it's going to be you who has to do it. And sometimes the bag is going to break. But if you're lucky, the bag won't break, and you'll come back from the curb just as clean as when you went out there. And maybe when you're out there at the curb, you will look up at the moon and stars, and the night air will be full of the smell of new flowers just opening in the spring. Maybe you will say a little prayer right then and there: "Dear God, thank You for the garbage. If it weren't for my job of taking it out, I would never have seen this wonderful sight." Maybe that's what you will say.... No, I don't really think so. Taking out the garbage never gets *that* good.

Look Both Ways Before You Cross the Street

Most of the things on The List are there to keep you safe. When your parents tell you, "Look both ways before you cross the street," it's mostly a safety thing. It goes with other safety items like: Don't lick the floor, Don't use somebody else's toothbrush, Don't jump around like a wild animal, and Don't touch, eat, or play with anything sharp, hot, slimy, smelly, broken, bloody, or dead. Steer clear of that stuff, and you will be safe most of the time.

Looking both ways before you cross the street is a way to keep you safe. That's why your parents are always nagging you about this when you are young. When you were little, your parents could keep you safe by keeping you close, but as you get older, your parents have to let you go. When they do, you have to know how to be careful yourself.

"Look both ways before you cross the street" is also supposed to teach you a deeper lesson: *Don't jump into things.* Looking both ways before you cross the street also means that you should not dive into water when you don't know how deep it is. You shouldn't go someplace with someone you haven't met before, and you shouldn't eat something that looks like it's still alive. It means that before you ask for a dog, you better look at all the hard things you have to do to take care of a dog. Once you look both ways, you might be willing to settle for a goldfish.

Now, looking both ways doesn't mean that you should be so frightened of being hurt that you won't want to cross the street at all. Our world is not just dangerous and scary but also fun and exciting. There is violence in the world, but there is also great adventure. One of the real hard things your parents have to do is scare you enough to keep you safe but not scare you so much that you never want to leave your room.

So understand that "Look both ways before you cross the street" means that you should stop, you should look both ways, but then, if there are no cars coming, you should go ahead and cross that street! It's a big wide world out there waiting to greet you, but you have to get safely across the street before you can say hello.

KEEP YOUR SHOES OFF THE COUCH

You probably don't even think much about the stuff on the bottom of your shoes. There's probably squashed bug guts, old scummy gum, melted ice cream, goop, spit, rotted leaves, stones, maybe some doggie poop, and stuff that only God knows what it is. If you looked at the bottom of your shoes with a microscope, you would probably throw up. You would see every kind of germ and bug and tiny gross crawly thing that lives there.

Once you think about the stuff on the bottom of your shoes, you can understand why putting your feet on the couch is such a bad idea. The stuff from your shoe bottoms can get smeared all over the place where you put your real bottom, and that is not a real good idea. Sitting on squashed bug guts is something most people don't want to do, and cleaning squashed bug guts off the living room couch is not something your folks should have to do. If you just keep your shoes on the floor, everything will stay clean, and that's the little reason why "Keep your

shoes off the couch" got on The List.

The big reason why "Keep your shoes off the couch" is on The List is so that you can learn one big word: *Respect!* Keeping your shoes off the couch is a way of showing respect for your parents, who worked hard to get the money to buy the couch. It's a way of showing respect for the people who have to clean the couch. It's a way of showing respect for the people who have no room to sit down if you are spread out all over the couch. Shoes and couches are little things, but respect is a big thing. Keeping your feet off the couch is a way of showing respect for all the people around you who got you both the shoes and the couch and who would like to share it with you (the couch, that is, not the shoes).

Did you know that, traditionally, Japanese people take off their shoes before they enter a house? Muslims take off their shoes before they go into a mosque to pray. God even told Moses to take off his shoes when Moses got near the burning bush. Now, if taking off shoes is good enough for Japanese people and for Muslim people and for Moses, it should be good enough for you. Of course, if you are a Japanese Muslim named Moses, you already know this. Taking off your shoes is a sign of respect. It's a sign that you know where you should go and where your shoes should go and that there are some places that both you and your shoes should never go near.

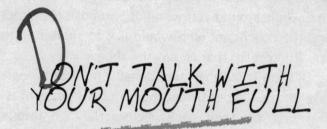

DON'T TALK WITH YOUR MOUTH FULL

Some things are bad because they are just bad, and some things are bad because they're just gross. Stealing and killing, hitting and hurting are bad because they are bad. Picking your nose and spitting, farting, and swearing are things that are bad because they're gross. Talking with your mouth full is probably one of the first gross things you learned how to do, and that's why telling you not to talk with your mouth full is probably one of the first things your parents told you not to do.

Gross things always look worse to other people than they do to the person doing them, so if you don't know how gross you look when you are talking with your mouth full, just do it in front of a mirror, and you'll see what you're making other people see. There is nothing you have to say that is so important that people need to hear it while your mouth is full of potatoes and peas. (Talking with your mouth full can also send food spit flying into another person's face, which is especially bad if you ever want that person to drive you to the movies.)

Your parents tell you that talking with your mouth full isn't good manners. You may say, "So what? Who cares about good manners? Manners are just about which fork to use, and who cares about that anyway?" Well, good manners are not just fork rules. Good manners keep our lives from getting mean and gross and ugly and selfish. But the even bigger reason for not talking with your mouth full is: *You need to learn to do just one thing at a time.*

Nobody can do lots of things at one time and do them all well. You can't do your homework and also watch television, because your attention will be swinging back and forth between your books and the tube, and you won't be able to concentrate on your work. You can't ride a bike and also listen to music on a Walkman, because you might not hear someone yelling to you, "Hey—watch out for the elephant!" Doing one thing well is hard enough; doing lots of things well all at once is almost impossible—especially with elephants around!

So slow down. Stop moving so fast. Eat, swallow, and *then* talk. You'll be surprised how many more people will want to hear what you have to say.

MONEY DOESN'T GROW ON TREES, YOU KNOW

Do you know how much things cost?

I know you see price tags on the things you want, but that's not *really* what those things cost. What something really costs is how hard you have to work to get it. So when you ask your folks for a new bike or a CD or new sneakers, you should know what they really cost. That new bike might cost your dad three hours of sitting in a traffic jam waiting to get to work. That CD might mean that your mom has to work an extra hour or two at her job. Those new sneakers might cost your folks eating dinner at home for two weeks instead of going out to eat at a restaurant. Things don't just cost money; they cost what you have to do to get the money.

This is why when you start asking for a lot of money to buy a lot of things, you'll hear this famous but silly-sounding thing on The List: "Money doesn't grow on trees, you know." When you first hear this, you might think your parents are kind of goofy  for telling you such an obvious thing. What they mean, of course, is that you should not think that it's as easy to get money as it is to pick apples off a tree. They want to teach you to respect the value of money.

When you're a kid, it's not your fault if you don't know what things cost. Most kids think everything is free or that you get as much money as you want from those cash machines. Another thing that makes it hard for kids to learn what things cost is advertising. When you are a kid, you watch lots of television commercials that try to get you to ask your parents to buy you some cereal or some toy or something. Those ads never tell you what the cereal or toys or things cost. So be careful. Just because something is on television doesn't make it worth the price.

The big meaning of "Money doesn't grow on trees, you know" is: *You need to learn what things really cost.* Most of the people with the most money worked very hard to get that money. Most of the people who can do most of the things you admire worked very hard for lots of hours to be able to do those things. Nothing is a free ride. Everything costs something.

Once you learn what things really cost, you will be able to make good decisions about whether you want to pay the price. If being popular at your school means that you have to do drugs, you should decide that it's too big a price to pay. If getting real good at gymnastics or skating or tennis means that you have to get up real early every day to practice before school, you may decide that it's too big a price to pay. Some grown-ups have decided that if making a lot of money in a job means that they can never really spend time with their family, it's too big a price to pay.

Some people believe that even though you need some money, the best things in life are free. Love, friendship, running, laughing, thinking up stuff, and dreaming are all free. Other people believe that—as the old song goes—even if the best things in life are free, you can give those things to the birds and bees. They want MONEY! That's what they want. What do *you* want?

Share your toys

Think about your favorite stuff. Think about your teddy bear that you've had forever that's real soft and kind of bare in spots. Think of the necklace your grandma gave you that you still wear. Think of your baseball glove with the perfect pocket or about your favorite video game—the one where you zap the cave monsters—or about your pocketknife with the tweezers and seventeen other tools in it. It's good to have favorite stuff.

Now think about your favorite people. Think about your family: your mom and your dad, your grandma and grandpa, your brothers and sisters and uncles and aunts and cousins. Think about your best friend who is always there for you. Think about the funny but nice mailman who waves to you, or the old lady in the bakery who always gives you a broken cookie for free. It's good to have favorite people.

Now think about this question: Are favorite people better than favorite stuff? I think so, because people can love you and stuff can't. Even your teddy bear, who looks like he loves you, is just a bit of cloth and stuffing. One of the very big lessons that all happy and wise people learn as they grow up is this: *People are better than stuff.* Another reason having stuff doesn't make you happy is that getting stuff and fixing stuff and storing stuff and insuring stuff and replacing old, worn-out stuff all takes time and more stuff.

Of course, you need some stuff. You need a house and food and clothes and some way to listen to music. But the amount of stuff that some people have and the amount of stuff that some people want is just ridiculous! Some people who have lots of money are starting to buy a lot less stuff and starting to give away some of the stuff they already have because they want to spend more time with the people they love and less time with the stuff they own.

The way your parents try to teach you that people are more important than stuff is to tell you to share your toys. Toys are stuff for kids. The problem with toys is that to really have fun, you need somebody to play with you and your toys, but if you don't share your toys, nobody will want to play with you. Then you'll be left all alone sitting on a pile of your toy stuff. That's exactly the way some grown-ups live, because they never learned to share their toys when they were kids.

Sharing your toys is the first time in your life that you get to feel how good it is to share and how bad it feels to be selfish. Sharing is easy when you get used to it, but it's hard if you never get used to it, so it's good to start learning to share when you're young and have some toys.

It's good to share your advice and your time. It's good to share your money and your food, it's good to share your love and your trust, and it all starts with sharing your toys. Once you learn to share, everything else is a piece of cake. Oh, and by the way, don't forget to share your cake, too!

TIE YOUR SHOES

There are two ways to finish something. You can *really* finish it or you can *sort of* finish it. You know how it is. If you are getting dressed, and you have a shoelace or two untied, and your shirt is not tucked in, and your hair is not combed, you are only *sort of* dressed. You are *really* dressed only when you are tied and tucked and combed and buttoned and zipped and brushed.

You can *sort of* clean your room, which happens when you scrape away the top layer of toys and games and dirty socks, or you can *really* clean your room, which happens only when the bed is made, your desk is cleaned, and you can see most of the floor. You can *sort of* set the table by throwing silver-ware and plates and glasses on the table, or you can *really* set the table by putting the knife on the right side and the fork and spoon on the left. (Or does the spoon go on the right?) And by neatly folding each napkin so it looks like a swan (all right, that's a little much). The point is that you can do anything two ways: *sort of* and *really.*

When your folks nag you to tie your shoes, they are doing it to keep you from tripping over your laces, falling down, and breaking your face. But they are also trying to teach you this: *You should finish what you start.* They want you to learn how to live *really* and not just *sort of.* They want you to learn that when you do a job, you should do it the best you can, not the fastest you can. Living *really* is much harder than living *sort of,* but it is much better, and one way you learn that is by tying your shoes.

Look around at the people who are really good at what they do. All of them are great shoe tiers. All of them have learned how to really finish what they start. These people don't do better than other people because they are better than other people. They do better because they work harder than other people. They do better because they never fool themselves into thinking that something is done before it is really done. They are never satisfied with the *sort of.* They are always looking for the *really.*

They are the people everybody else goes to when

they want something to get really done. When your folks nag you about tying your shoes, it is because they want you to be one of those people. It's not that they care so much about you tripping up on the street. It's that they care a lot about you tripping up in life. So tie your shoes, put the spoon to the right of the knife, and finish what you start—and you will be just fine...really!

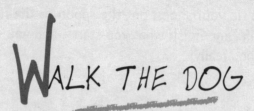

WALK THE DOG

You get to pee and poop pretty much whenever you want, but your dog isn't so lucky. Some dogs have to wait all day for somebody to come home and take them for a pee and poop walk. That's the first reason you should walk your dog. Walking the dog is something your dog *really* needs! Dogs don't need much: food, exercise, a few things, to chew on, someplace warm and dry to sleep, and someone to play with. If you give your dog those things, it will love you forever.

People need a lot more care than dogs. People need everything dogs need *plus* birthday presents and phone calls, clothes and kisses, books and games, music and cake. It's just a lot harder to take care of a person than it is to take care of a dog. That's why it's a good idea to start learning how to take care of living things by beginning with a dog.

Dogs need to be walked no matter what the weather is like and no matter how tired you are from doing other things. That's a big lesson you can learn by walking your dog: *You have to take care of the ones you love, no matter what!* The people and living things you love are depending on you to take care of them, and when you do it, you have learned responsibility. Responsibility is doing the right things for the ones who depend on you. Being responsible and doing the right thing and taking care of the ones you love is the only way to show that you really do love them.

You just can't love something and then not take care of it. Parents who say they love their kids but don't take care of them when they are young really don't love them. Kids who say they love their parents but don't take care of them when they get old really don't love them. Love is not just what we feel. Love is what we do!

Always say please and thank you

Think about the real bad people you know. Not the ones on the evening news who just killed somebody or set off a bomb, but the little bad people you know in your life—the bullies, the liars, the cheaters, the kids who steal lunch money or write on the walls.

Now think about how these people you know got bad.

I bet most of them got bad in little ways before they got bad in big ways. And if they keep going getting worse, maybe someday they will end up on the evening news too. The people who steal cars started out by stealing candy bars. The people who shoot other people started out by hitting other people. The people who cheat in business started out by cheating in school. That's how people go bad.

The other way is also true. People who end up being good in big ways started out by learning to be good in little ways. People who save other people from burning buildings started out by helping old people across the street. People who give away a lot of money to charity began by giving away a few pennies to charity when they were kids. People who help the world began by learning to help the person right next door.

Because getting good or getting bad happen the same way, one little step at a time, your parents will always be on your case to do nice little things. They know that if they can get you to do the nice little things when you are young, the nice big things will come naturally to you when you grow up. And one of the main little things your parents will probably tell you to do is, "Say please and thank you."

Saying please shows that you are not piggy or selfish, but are willing to wait and ask for what you want. *Please* shows that you know that the person does not have to give you what you want.

Saying thank you shows that you are grateful for what you get. *Thank you* shows that you know that you are real lucky to get most of the things you get. *Please* and *thank you* may seem like little words, but saying them shows that you are really a very big person.

If you forget to say please and thank you, your parents may ask you, "What do you say?" This is not really a question but an order. It's their soft way of ordering you to say please or thank you (whichever one you forgot). Being asked, "What do you say?" is better than being told, "Say please!" or "Say thank you!" "What do you say?" is your last chance to show that you are not a total jerk.

The big meaning of "please" and "thank you" is this: *Everything you get is a gift.* All of us sometimes get the bad idea that what we get is owed to us. Kids who think that their parents and the world owe them everything turn into selfish, spoiled people. So try to think of what you get as stuff you didn't deserve but got anyway because somebody loved you and wanted to give you something nice. If you think that way about what you get, you will never get selfish.

If you get into the habit of always saying please and thank you to other people, you will find it real easy to say please and thank you to God. And then it will be real easy to thank God for your life, which is the biggest gift of all.

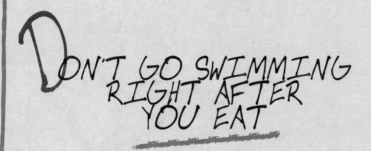DON'T GO SWIMMING RIGHT AFTER YOU EAT

Some of the things on The List are not true, but they are still on The List. One of these is "Don't go swimming right after you eat." For years, millions of parents told zillions of kids (including me) that if you went swimming right after you ate, you would get cramps and sink to the bottom of the pool or the lake like a stone.

No parents ever doubted this thing on The List. The only thing parents argued about was *how long* their kid had to wait. Maybe you had ten-minute parents, who would let you go into the water only ten minutes after scarfing down your hot dog and soda. Maybe you had half-hour parents. I had *one-hour* parents, and I hated it.

Well, now it turns out that the whole thing about eating and waiting and swimming and cramps is not true! You don't need to wait at all before you go swimming after you eat (except of course to avoid peeing in the pool, which we talked about in another chapter). The fact is, hot-dog-eating swimmers don't get cramps any more than non–hot-dog-eating swimmers!

Now, the strange thing is that even though "Don't go swimming right after you eat" isn't true, it's still on The List. I heard some mother say it to a kid just last week at a pool. I didn't say anything, but I felt sorry for the kid. Then I realized that cramping was just the little meaning of "Don't go swimming right after you eat." The big meaning has nothing to do with cramps and is still very true and very important.

The big meaning is: *You need to learn how to wait.*

Waiting is one of the things that most adults know how to do and most kids don't. If you think I'm wrong, just remember the last long car trip you took with your family. I bet that after just a few minutes, you or your little brother or sister started to ask, "Are we there yet?" And I also bet that this question got asked a zillion times before you got to where you were going.

There are lots of things you need to learn to wait for. You need to wait until you know enough to get a job before you leave school. You need to wait until you are old enough to know what being married really means before you get married. You need to wait to drive, or vote, or drink, or go on the really, really scary rides at the amusement park. You need to wait to have sex. There are lots of things you need to wait to do, and the reason is that you are just not big enough, or strong enough, or mature enough, or educated enough yet to do them in the right way. When your parents tell you to wait after you eat before you go swimming, they are just getting you ready to wait for all these good things.

Most people who live a happy life are good waiters. Good scientists know how to wait for their discoveries. Good business people know how to wait for their businesses to grow. People who want to be the president know how to wait for their chance. But waiting doesn't mean that you'll always get what you want, even after you wait. Sometimes scientists work their whole lives and never find what they're looking for. Sometimes people work hard and wait to be the president of something, and their chance never comes. Waiting doesn't mean you will get what you want, but *not* waiting almost always means that you *won't* get what you want.

If you can't learn this from your parents, go watch a baseball game. In baseball the time you spend waiting is much more than the time you spend playing. You wait for the batter to get set, and you wait for the pitcher to pitch, and you wait for the batter to hit the ball. In baseball you wait a lot, but then— *smack!*—something happens, and you have to be prepared to make the play. Baseball is like life. Lots of waiting and then something happens fast. So get ready, get set, and...wait (but now maybe you can wait *in* the pool).

IF YOU CAN'T SAY ANYTHING NICE, DON'T SAY ANYTHING AT ALL

I bet you have been hurt the most by words, not by sticks and stones. Words hurt more than a punch, but words can heal much better than medicine. Words can lift you up or smash you down; words can make you hated or make you loved. Words can build up somebody's good name or tear it down. Once you understand how much words can hurt, you'll want to stick with words that heal.

Most people talk too much, a few people talk too little, and hardly any people talk just the right amount. What matters is not how much you say but how much nice stuff you say. And here is the big secret of life here on earth: The more nice things you say, the more nice things you will see.

Saying nothing is so much better than saying something hurtful or angry or bad. Saying nothing gives you time to cool down. Saying nothing gives you time to figure out why you're so angry. Saying nothing keeps you from saying something you can never take back. You can't get into trouble for something you never say.

"If you can't say anything nice, don't say anything at all" is one of the oldest and maybe the most famous sayings on The List. The little reason it's on The List is to teach you the power of words and to teach you to use your words carefully. But the big meaning of "If you can't say anything nice, don't say anything at all" is real big: *You need to praise others just as much as you need to be praised.*

All of us human beings need to hear good things about ourselves so that we can believe good things about ourselves. That's how we're built. If we're never praised, we feel like scum. If we're praised, we feel like real decent people. Once you understand just how important it is to be praised, you will find it a lot easier to praise other people. When somebody you know does something good, tell him or tell her. It will make you feel good, but it will make that other person feel terrific.

Here's the problem. There will be times in your life when you need somebody to say something nice about you, but nobody will be saying anything at all.

Maybe it happens this way: When nobody is saying anything nice about you here on earth, God and the angels may be talking about you in heaven. Maybe they are talking about how special you are and about all the blessings you have and will bring to others. Maybe when nobody is cheering for you here, everybody is cheering for you there.

So, go out there and help God and the angels in heaven cheer up somebody here on earth by saying something nice. They can use all the help they can get.

I'M GONNA COUNT TO THREE AND THEN...

You know how dynamite goes off? You light a fuse and it burns closer and closer to the dynamite until...KABOOM! When your parents say, "I'm gonna count to three and then...," you should know that they are close to KABOOM! "I'm gonna count to three and then..." is a parent fuse. Its little meaning is that the fuse is lit, the clock is ticking, and your life is about to be not as much fun as it is now.

What happens after the counting and after the KABOOM depends on what you did and on how long a fuse your parents have. Sometimes the KABOOM ends with "You can't watch television for a week," or "You can't use the telephone for a week," or "You're grounded." An average KABOOM could get you grounded for a day or two. A big KABOOM might get you grounded for a week or two. I remember causing KABOOMs in my house where I thought I would be grounded until I got married and moved away.

Whatever happens *after* the KABOOM is not that important. What is important is this: *You need to hear the counting before the KABOOM.* If you hear your parents counting, you can stop what you are doing or do what you are *not* doing, and that will stop the KABOOM.

There is always a sign of trouble coming. There is always some way to know, before it is too late, that you have gone too far. You just have to learn to listen. If you've hurt a friend and, when you see him, he walks away from you, the walking away is the counting before the KABOOM. If you're kidding around with somebody and you see her get a tear in her eye, then what you think is just kidding around is really hurting her feelings. That tear is the counting before the KABOOM. If you don't do your homework and your teacher takes a deep breath and shakes his head, that breath and that shake is the counting before the KABOOM.

You can stop most of the KABOOMs that will happen in your life if you just learn to listen. Hearing that counting could even save someone in trouble— including yourself. So learn to listen to the counting, or get ready for the KABOOM!

DON'T TALK TO YOUR FATHER/MOTHER LIKE THAT

Curse words are not the only bad words you know. "Oh yeah?" is right up there with swearing. The "Oh yeah?" I mean is the "Oh yeah?" you say when your parents have told you to do something and you couldn't care less, or you want to show them that they better not mess with you. That "Oh yeah?" moves you across the line from doing something lazy to doing something bad.

Mouthing off to your parents can happen many ways. You don't have to say "Oh yeah?" or swear. There are many ways you can show disrespect to your parents, and all of them are bad. It's bad when you tell hurtful jokes about your parents. It's bad when you ignore your parents when they're talking to you. And it's very bad when you hit your parents. And if you do mouth off to one parent and your other parent is there, that parent is going to say, "Don't talk to your father [or mother] like that!"

It's bad to mouth off to anybody, but it's especially bad to mouth off to your parents. And that's an important meaning here: Your parents deserve special respect. Your parents are the ones who are giving up time and money to raise you. Your parents are the ones who love you more than anybody on this earth. Your parents are the ones who are trying to teach you The  List and how you can be a good person. Your parents should be the most important people in your life. If you can't treat your parents with respect, nobody else you meet in your life will be safe.

That's the big thing: *All people deserve to be talked to and treated with kindness and appreciation.* All people are like you, and people are as close to God as we can get. So when you trash another person, it's almost like trashing God. Maybe it would be a good idea for you to practice seeing God's face in the faces of all the people you meet. Let's try to treat each other the way we would treat God if we could meet God (which we can't until we die, and there is no need to rush that!).

So just remember to talk to everybody with respect—and when you're talking to your parents, *extra* respect is a good idea. Just think of all the diapers they changed for you. Think of all the booboos they bandaged for you. Think of all the times you threw up on them. Think of all the stormy nights when they stayed with you in your room until you fell asleep. People who did that for you deserve a lifetime of respect. Even if they had only changed your diapers and let you puke on them, they would deserve that respect!

CLEAN YOUR PLATE

The way you will probably hear "Clean your plate!" from your folks is something like this: "There are starving children in [then your parents will fill in the name of a starving country—when I was growing up, it was China] who would give their left arm [some parents use the right arm] for this food, so clean your plate!"

Now, when you hear this, you probably shouldn't say, "Okay, send them my left arm. I'm not eating the broccoli casserole!" Being a wise guy to your parents is not a good idea, and cleaning your plate is a good idea for a whole bunch of reasons.

The first reason it's good to eat all the food on

your plate is that throwing away food that costs money and takes time to cook is wasteful. It's amazing how when you move out of the house and have to buy and cook your own food it's suddenly so easy to become a member of the Clean Plate Club. (You see, if you *do* eat everything on your plate, then your parents make a big deal about how you are now a member of the Clean Plate Club, which as far as I can tell is not a real club and has no meetings and no members!)

Food is not just fuel for your body. Food is a blessing, a blessing on a plate. Food comes from the many people who grow it and pick it and ship it and sell it, but food mainly comes from God, who made this world just right for growing food. That's why lots of people stop before they eat to say a prayer of thanks to God, who put that food on that plate in the *big* way, not the little ways.

Even if you are not a praying kind of person, cleaning your plate is a way to remember this lesson: *Be grateful for what you have.* Every night on this planet over two hundred million children go to bed hungry. What's worse, forty thousand children die *every day* because they have had no food to eat for many days. And you shouldn't think that all these hungry children live in Africa or Asia or some other faraway place. Over twelve million children right here in the good old U.S. of A. are undernourished. Some of these kids might live in your town or in the town next door to your town.

So one big thing you can learn from cleaning your plate is to do something so that other kids who are hungry can get something on their plates tonight. Maybe you can get together with other people to help deliver food to hungry people or serve food in a soup kitchen, or maybe you could give money to places that are doing this. Maybe you could even find some great new way to help hungry people get fed.

And while you are thinking about what you can do to relieve the hunger in the world, remember the difference between heaven and hell. In hell, you see, hungry people are sitting around a table loaded with wonderful food. They can see the food and smell the food and touch the food, but they can't eat the food, because their arms don't bend and they can't bring the food to their mouths. That's hell.

In heaven hungry people are sitting around a table loaded with wonderful food. They can see the food and smell the food and touch the food, but they can't eat the food, because their arms don't bend and they can't bring the food to their mouths. That's heaven.

So what's the difference between heaven and hell? That's easy. In heaven the people are feeding one another.

Do YOUR HOMEWORK

There is a reason they call it homework. Lots of work we do has to get done at home even before we get to school or to work. School is not just for teaching you stuff. School is also for checking up on the stuff you taught yourself at home.

The kids who do best in school are not the ones who kiss up to the teacher, or the ones who are the most popular, or the ones who join the most clubs. The kids who do best in school are the ones who do their homework. They are the ones who understand that learning means practicing what somebody told you, and it means thinking about what somebody told you, and it means reading things somebody told you to read, and all these things happen at home rather than school.

Now, as you grow up, you will soon learn that kids who did their homework do better when they get out of school than kids who didn't do their homework. The people who do best don't just go to their jobs; they get ready for their jobs. These are the people who go home and think and plan and get new ideas, which they bring to work with their lunch the next day. These are the people who have learned the big lesson of homework: *Prepare for everything you do*. So that's why your folks are always on you about doing your homework—they want you to learn how to know what's going on before it goes on. To be that kind of person, there are no shortcuts. You need to do your homework.

Now, there will be times in your life when you need help with your homework. That's okay. That's normal. Some people need more help than other people, everybody learns in his or her own way, but everybody needs help to learn. Learning how to get help is really one of the biggest parts of homework.

But letting somebody else do your homework is a bad deal. If other people do your homework for you, it's just a form of cheating, and they are helping a cheater, which is almost as bad as being a cheater. If you let your parents help you with your homework, that's fine, but if you let your parents make the papier-mâché map of Italy you were supposed to make for social studies, that's not fine. They will be cheating you out of the chance to learn how to do it yourself.

Then later in your life, let's say you are trying to get hired as the president of a big company, and you have a real good chance to get the job. At the last interview let's say they sit you down and say to you, "We like you a lot, and we would really like to hire you for this big job, but there is just one more thing we would like you to do. Could you just make us a papier-mâché map of Italy?"

And you will have to say to all those people, "I'm sorry, but, you see, when I was in fourth grade I had a homework assignment to make a papier-mâché map of Italy for Ms. Donat's social studies class, but my mom made the map for me so I never learned how."

And then they will say, "Too bad. You can't be president of our company. Good-bye."

This happens a lot.

Do your homework!

Cover Your Mouth When You Sneeze

Right now bad germs are trying to get you.

Your body is like a spaceship, and the bad germs are like the space aliens trying to get inside. The bad germs come from the air you breathe, and from the water you drink, and from the food you eat. Most of the time these bad germs get stopped by the bad-germ fighters in your body, but sometimes they get through, and that's when you get sick. It's amazing how God made our bodies so they could fight bad germs so well. Even when the bad germs do get into you, the bad-germ fighters never stop fighting to make you well again.

One of the big ways the bad germs get inside of

you is by surfing a sneeze. The bad germs have little tiny surfboards that ride on sneeze drops, and when you sneeze, you give the germs in you a ride on your sneeze drops. Sneeze drops are real little, and they can stay in the air for a long time, and if somebody breathes in your sneeze drops, your germs surf right into them and start to make them sick. This is why your folks are always telling you, "Cover your mouth when you sneeze." They don't want you to give any of your bad germs a real easy way to get into anybody else's body.

You're going to sneeze on other people if you go out of the house in the morning without sneeze protection. So you should always take paper tissues or a handkerchief with you. Then when you feel a sneeze coming on, you will be able to reach for something to cover your mouth. Sneezes usually give you a little time before they go off, but if you aren't carrying any sneeze protection, you don't have a chance, and it will be surf city for all your bad germs.

You don't need to sneeze on somebody else to hurt them, and that is the big meaning of "Cover your mouth when you sneeze": *Don't hurt anybody, even in little ways.* You should watch out that nothing you do makes somebody else feel bad or silly, sick or sad. Maybe you are not spreading germs, but you are spreading gossip or hurtful jokes or lies, and that's just as bad. Gossiping is like sneezing on someone with words. In fact, gossiping or saying bad things about other people is worse than sneezing on them, because bad germs go away much faster than bad words.

And by the way, when somebody sneezes, the right thing to say is "God bless you" (or maybe "Gesundheit," which is a German word that means "Stay healthy"). If other people are ready to bless you when you sneeze, the least you can do is be ready to bless them by covering your mouth!

STAND UP STRAIGHT

When you think about the really bad things you can do in your life, slouching is not even in the top ten. So when your parents nag you and tell you to stand up straight, you may be thinking, So what! There are wars all over the world, kids are sick, and the Mets look like they'll never win another game, and with all that going on, all you can do is nag me about my posture! Give me a break. You should be happy I'm standing up at all.

Well, let's just take a minute and think about posture before you give your "Give me a break!" speech to your mom and dad. One big reason standing up straight is important is that standing up straight gives all your insides enough room to slosh around and do their job. You see, squashed things don't work as well as unsquashed things, and when you slouch, your insides get squashed. Your stomach goes into your lungs, your lungs go into your throat, and your throat goes into your head, and really, when you think about it, who wants a throat in his or her head. Standing up straight helps give your insides the space to work right.

But standing up straight is about a lot more than your insides. It didn't get on The List because our parents are posture freaks. When you are told to stand up straight, your parents are really trying to teach you this: *Show everyone that you believe in yourself.* Standing up straight makes you look like you have confidence. Standing up straight makes you look proud. Standing up straight sends the message that no matter how many people give up on you, you won't give up on yourself.

Slouching is your body's way of showing that you are feeling low, just like smiling is your body's way of showing that you are feeling happy. It's strange how the way you look on the outside can show just exactly how you're feeling on the inside. But maybe you're thinking, Some days I just don't feel proud or good or confident or happy. It would be a lie for me to stand up straight. Why can't I slouch on those days?

I know how you feel, but even on those days, it's good to stand up straight, because even on your worst days, you're still terrific. You're a good person with a bright future, and people love you and believe in you and want you to be the very best you can be. All those people who love you can't be wrong! They must see something in you that on your bad days you can't even see in yourself.

So on the bad days, try to stand up straight and try to believe in yourself. You may even find that your terrible day turns into just a bad day. That may not seem to be much of an improvement, but in this world and in this life on this planet in this solar system in this galaxy, sometimes it's the best we can do. Lots of things in your life will try to squash you. There is just no good reason to squash yourself.

SAY YOU'RE SORRY

If you want to grow up to be a good person you only have two choices:

Choice #1: You can learn how to never do anything bad.

Choice #2: You can learn how to say I'm sorry.

Since choice #1 is impossible, you better think hard about choice #2.

Saying you're sorry shows great things about you. It shows that you know you did something wrong. It shows that you can admit to others that you did it. And it shows that you're trying to change so that you don't do it again. All those are great things to say about you, and that's why when you don't say

I'm sorry, your parents will nag you to say it.

Saying you're sorry is not only good for you, it's also good for the person you hurt. When you hurt somebody else, you can't take back the hurt. You can erase a mistake on a piece of paper, and you can delete a mistake on a computer screen, but people are not paper or computers. When you hurt another person, that person stays hurt until you do something to take away the hurt.

And the only way to take away the hurt is to go right up to the person as soon as you can and say to him or to her, "I hurt you, and I'm sorry. I wish I didn't do it, but I did it. I hope you can forgive me, because if you did it to me, I would forgive you." When you can say that, you will have learned the big lesson behind "Say you're sorry," and that lesson is: *You need to fix up what you mess up.*

You should know that some I'm sorry's are cheap. These are the I'm sorry's you say when you don't mean it. Lots of times your parents make you say you're sorry when you're still real angry, and you're not sorry for anything, but you have to say it because your mom is pulling you by the ear. Everybody can tell when you say a cheap I'm sorry, but here's the thing: Even a cheap I'm sorry is better than no I'm sorry at all, because even if you don't mean the right thing, at least you said the right thing. You can work on meaning it later.

Another way an I'm sorry is cheap is if you say

you're sorry about something you did, but you don't try to fix what you did. If you steal something, you can't just say "I'm sorry" when you get caught. You have to give back what you stole. When you tell a lie, you can't just say "I'm sorry." You have to tell the truth. If you forget to invite somebody to your party, you can't just say "I'm sorry" to the person you didn't invite. You have to invite them the next time.

One more thing (and I'm sorry to have to tell you this, but it's the truth): When you say "I'm sorry" to the person you hurt, that person may still not forgive you. He or she may still be too hurt by what you did to say "That's okay." If that happens to you (and believe me, it's going to happen to you), you should say "I'm sorry" again and again. You don't have to say it forever, but you do have to say it more than once. Remember, you are the hurter, not the hurtee. If you say you're sorry to somebody a bunch of times and they still will not forgive you, then it's time to move on. What matters is that you tried to make things right. In life it's the trying that matters most.

DON'T JUDGE A BOOK BY ITS COVER

If you could choose between being really good-looking or really nice, what would you choose?

I hope you would choose nice, but I'm afraid that lots of kids would choose good-looking. I understand that. Good-looking people get treated better than people who are not that good-looking. Movie stars, models, the people who read the news on television, and the people who are on the covers of most of the magazines are mostly all good-looking. And in your school, I bet that the most popular kids are almost always the best-looking kids. I was not one of the best-looking kids in school. I was skinny. I had big black glasses, and I was born with a chest bone that was kind of sunken in. So on behalf of all the goofy-looking kids out there (which may include you), I have this to say about the way good-looking people are treated: IT'S JUST NOT FAIR!

You know and your folks know that the way good-looking people are treated isn't fair. Everybody except the good-looking people knows that it's not fair, and that's why "Don't judge a book by its cover" is on The List. It's the way your parents try to teach you that how you look on the inside is *much* more important than how you look on the outside.

Just like a book with a dull or ugly cover could be a great book, a person with a goofy look could be a great person. In fact, I think that your chances of becoming a great person are much better if you are not the best-looking kid in school. The reason for this is compassion. Ugly kids have an easier time becoming compassionate than beautiful kids. They know how it feels to be made fun of because of big ears, or zits, or frizzy hair, or being fat. When you feel the hurt of being made fun of, it's just a whole lot easier to learn how to feel the hurts of others.

It's hard to look beyond the cover of a book, and it's hard to look inside a beautiful person, but you have to try to do it. If you don't, you might get tricked and disappointed and hurt. Maybe somebody good-looking will seem to be your friend, or sell you something, or tell you to do something when all he or she is really trying to do is use you or make money off you or hurt you. The only way to be sure about people is to know how they treat others.

Now, I don't want you to get the idea that all beautiful people are selfish jerks. Some people who are real nice are also real beautiful. My best friend is a priest. He looks like a movie star, but he is also a terrific human being. Go figure!

So the big meaning of "Don't judge a book by its cover" is: *Look deeper*. If you're thinking about getting to know a person, look deeper than how they look. If you're thinking of buying something, look deeper than how it looks. If you're thinking about someone's ideas, look deeper than how well that person speaks. Life is complicated, but when you learn to look deeper, life gets a whole lot simpler. When you learn to look deeper, you will see the true beauty that God put in people and in the world. It's the kind of beauty that never goes away.

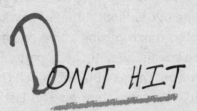

DON'T HIT

Getting hit by somebody is awful. I hope you have never been hit by anybody, but if it did happen to you, I hope it wasn't that bad, and I hope it didn't happen more than once. There are lots of bad things in the world, but I believe hitting is right up there near the top.

Lots of kids get hit, and lots of times the kids who get hit are the ones who hit other kids. The real bad thing is that some of these kids who get hit grow up to be adults who hit. You would think that kids who get hit would never want to hit anybody else, but it doesn't always work that way. Getting hit makes some kids so angry that they want to go out and hit somebody else. Hitting is like fire. Once you start it, you can't always control it.

This is why, if you hit, good parents are going to tell you in very strong words, *"Don't hit!"* What they're also saying is this: *There are lots of ways to work something out without hitting.* They know that there is just too much hitting going on these days, and they don't want you to be a part of it. They raised you to work things out, not punch things out.

"Don't hit" is a huge item on The List, but you would never know it if you go to the movies or watch a lot of television. You see too much hitting and hurting and exploding and shooting and knifing and killing on the tube and in the movies. You probably see a hundred murders a week on television, and that is about a hundred murders too many.

Now, you might say, "Hey, all that television and movie hitting is fake. It's just a movie. It's not real. Everybody knows that the girl who just got hit by the guy didn't really even get hit, and the guy who just got shot didn't really die. The bullets were fake, the blood was fake, and the screaming and yelling 'Please don't kill me!' was all fake. They just do it to make the movie or the television show more exciting. I won't do any of that stuff in my life ever."

Maybe that's what you say. But maybe you're wrong. Maybe, after seeing all this hitting and shooting and killing, deep down your brain will tell you this: "Hey, it's neat to chase other people and hurt them and blow them away. Doing that stuff shows that you're strong and that other people should be afraid of you and respect you, and it's good for other people to be afraid of you and respect you because then they won't mess with you."

If you get that message from all the hitting and hurting and chasing and blowing up you see on television and in the movies, you're going to be in big trouble, because as soon as you get angry with another kid, you might hit him or her instead of talking things over. After you learn that the first thing you do when you get angry is hit, you're in trouble—and the people around you are in trouble.

Once you learn that *talking*—not *hitting*—is the way to work out your problems, you will have learned one of the best and biggest lessons your parents could ever teach you. Then someday maybe you will be the president of the United States, and then you can teach that lesson about talking and not hitting to all the nations in the world that haven't learned it yet. And then you'll win some big peace prize, and then you'll have to give a speech. (Now, in that speech, please don't forget to remind everybody that you learned about not hitting from your folks, who learned it from The List.)

So give peace a chance. Don't hit!

DON'T COPY OFF YOUR NEIGHBOR

There are lots of ways to cheat but only one way to be honest. Your life will be a lot easier if you're honest, because then you only have to learn one way to be. One of your parents' and teachers' big jobs is teaching you to be honest, and one of the ways they do that is by being honest themselves so that you have a good example to follow. Another way they do it is by telling you not to copy off Jennifer Snouder's math quiz. Copying off another student's test is one of the ways that kids first learn to cheat.

If you do decide to be a cheater, you're going to have a lot of work to do. You're going to have to learn all the ways to cheat. Then you're going to have to learn all the ways to lie when you get caught. Most of all, you're going to have to figure out how to live with yourself, knowing that you're just a low-down dirty cheater. This is a lot to have to learn. It's just a whole lot simpler to learn to be honest.

There are lots of other things wrong with cheating besides the fact that it's just plain wrong. Cheating cheats you. If you're a cheater, you never learn what you can do all by yourself, so you never learn how to get better. Cheating makes other people mistrust you. If you are a cheater, you better start looking for other cheaters to make friends with, because no honest people want a cheater as a friend.

The other big lesson about not copying off your neighbor goes beyond being honest. By telling you not to copy off your neighbor's paper, your folks are trying to teach you not to copy your neighbor's clothes, or ideas, or life. If you live your life copying what other people do, you'll never find out the way that is right for you. If you copy the way other people dress, you'll never figure out what looks good on you. If you copy the way other people think, you'll never figure out what you really think. So not copying off your neighbor will help teach you this: *Find your own way in life.*

Here's what I think about cheating. It's a little weird, but it's what I believe. Maybe, just maybe, God counts up the cheaters and the honest folks every day. If there are more honest people in the world that day, *maybe* God decides to save the world, but if there are more cheaters, *maybe* God decides *not* to save the world. And maybe some days it's a tie! But maybe one day it'll be a tie between cheaters and honest people—until God counts *you.* If you're honest, the world gets saved, but if you're a cheater, the world gets wiped out.

Now, *if* this ever happens, you wouldn't want the whole world to go down the tubes just because you didn't know the answer to question number five on the math quiz and so you copied off Jennifer Snouder's math quiz, would you? *I don't think so!*

So the next time you are sitting there in class, and you don't know the answer to a question, and you have a chance to copy off your neighbor—FOR THE SAKE OF THE WHOLE WORLD, DON'T DO IT!

Copying off your neighbor starts with math quizzes, but it ends up in your life. It's hard enough to find your own way in life, but copying off your neighbor makes it even harder. So go out there, do your best, answer all the questions (or guess at them), but do it yourself, and forget about Jennifer Snouder. She was never that good in math anyway!

I HOPE THAT, WHEN YOU GROW UP, YOU'LL HAVE A KID JUST LIKE YOU

Your parents love you.

They always want what's best for you.

But sometimes you drive them crazy.

When you disobey them, or when you don't show respect for other people, or when you don't do your homework, or when you just act goofy, you may hear this famous item from The List: "I hope that when you grow up, you'll have a kid just like you!"

Of course your folks don't really want you to grow up and have a goofy, embarrassing kid. What they hope is that someday you'll be a parent, and someday your kid will act like you're acting at that moment, and then you'll understand just how frustrating it is to your parents for you to act that way.

If you just stop to think about how what you are doing looks to your parents, you might not do it in the first place. They want you to know how much it hurts them to have you act like you don't love them when they know that you really *do* love them. It's hard, but it's important to see things from your parents' point of view. That's the big meaning: *Put yourself in somebody else's shoes.*

Compassion is being able to feel what other people are feeling. Compassion means being able to get out of your own skin and your own feelings and your own life, and to feel what some other human being is feeling right now. Compassion is one of the very best things you can have as a grown-up human being, and the best way to practice compassion is by learning to feel what your parents are feeling, because you love them more than anybody.

Once you have compassion for your parents, you can have compassion for the whole rest of the world, one person at a time. If you have real compassion, you can feel what homeless people feel even if you are not homeless, you can feel what lost people feel even if you are not lost, you can feel what disabled people feel even if you are not disabled. And even better, there is joy and laughing and fun and whole new ways of looking at the world that will open up for you once you can get out of yourself and into the way the world looks to other people who are sharing this world with you right now.

So if you do become a compassionate person, I know that when you grow up, you *will* have a kid just like you!

Go GIVE GRANDMA A KISS

Maybe getting old is going to be good for you, or maybe getting old is going to be bad for you, but the one sure thing is that—with luck—getting old is going to happen to you! And when you do get old, one of the things that will make your life shine is getting a kiss from your grandson or granddaughter. When you don't get that kiss, you feel lousy. This is why when you go to visit your grandpa or grandma and you don't run right over and give them a big hug and a kiss, your parents will probably tell you, "Go give Grandma [or Grandpa] a kiss."

Maybe you don't want to run right over and kiss Grandma, because maybe your grandma smells! Old people can smell bad sometimes. It's not their fault. When you get old, your body just doesn't work the same way or smell the same way it did when you were young.

Maybe you don't want to kiss Grandma because her wrinkles feel funny. Your skin is smooth now, but it won't stay smooth forever. Skin usually gets wrinkled up as you get older. Your mom might be trying right now to get rid of some of the wrinkles in her face, but there is no way she can get skin as smooth as yours out of a bottle. The reason we get wrinkles is that as we get older, our insides shrink up, but our outsides don't. We have more skin than we need, and when we get old, the extra skin just kind of piles up.

I think that wrinkles are terrific, because they show what your face has been doing all your life. If your face has spent most of its time smiling, you will have smile wrinkles. If your face has spent most of its time frowning, you will have frown wrinkles. Smile wrinkles are one of the very best things people can have on their face.

So there is no reason not to run over and give your grandparents a big hug and kiss as soon as you see them. Your grandparents are the reason your parents are here, and your parents are the reason *you* are here. So by giving your grandparents hugs and kisses, you're saying thank you for your life.

When your parents tell you to give Grandma a

kiss, it's also to teach you this: *You need to respect age.* We live in a world where lots of people think that new is good and old is bad. Because of this idea, when some people get old, they don't think that they're important or useful or good anymore. Your kiss reminds your grandma or grandpa that they're still loved and still important and still one of the very best things in your life.

Just remember that old people have lived a long time, and there are certain things in life that just take a whole lot of time to learn. Young people may be fast and smart, but old people are slow and wise. It's good to be slow and wise. When I was young, I didn't think so, but as I get older it makes sense to me. So go give Grandma a kiss, and if she is not near you now, call her up and kiss her over the phone.

CALL IF YOU'RE GOING TO BE LATE

Think about all the good things you have in your life because you're a part of a family. More than the toys and clothes and CDs and trips and balls and racquets and gum—more than *all* the stuff you get— you get something much more important: *You get loved.* Getting loved is the most important thing you can get in this world, and you get it from your family.

Have you ever thought about the price of love? Have you ever thought about what you owe your folks for loving you? Cleaning up your room isn't the real price of love, even though you should clean up your room for the people who love you. Helping with the dishes, or taking out the garbage, or walking the dog—none of your chores around the house is the price of love. Calling if you're going to be late—now *that's* the price of love!

Calling if you're going to be late is the way you tell your folks not to worry about you when you don't come home at the time you said. That's the little meaning. The real little meaning is that you don't want your folks to worry about you, and then get angry at you, and then ground you for the rest of the school year because you made them worry. Not getting grounded is the little reason a lot of kids do a lot of things.

The big reason you should call if you're going to be late is: *What you do affects everybody who loves you.* Calling shows that you know that you're a part of a family that loves you. It's a way of saying to your folks that even though you're out with your friends doing something that is fun for you, you're still thinking about them and about how much you love them. It's a way of thanking your parents for trusting you and showing them that they're trusting the right person.

Sometimes it's hard to get to a phone to call home. Tough! Do it anyway! You should never think that it's a small thing to call home. Your parents will probably not be able to sleep until they hear you coming through the front door. That's the price your parents pay for loving you, and calling if you're going to be late is the price you pay for loving them. Isn't it a little price to pay for being a part of a family that loves you and will be waiting for you always? Besides...it will help your parents get some sleep.

DO AS I SAY, NOT AS I DO

Think about your best teachers. Not just your teachers at school but the people who have taught you the most about life. I bet all of them have something in common. I bet that all of them did what they told you to do. If you had a teacher who taught you how good it was to read books, I bet that teacher read a lot of books. If there was somebody who taught you to be kind to animals, I bet that teacher was real kind to animals, too. If somebody taught you to be honest, I bet he or she was honest, too. The best teachers you'll ever have do what they teach.

But not always.

Sometimes you will have teachers who don't always do the right thing, even if they are trying to teach you the right thing. The problem is simple. Nobody's perfect. Not you, not your mom, not your dad, not Grandpa or Grandma—not nobody!

Even the best people, people like your mom and dad, occasionally do the wrong thing even when they know the right thing. Sometimes you might even catch them doing it. When you catch your folks or your teachers doing a bad thing and you say something about it to them, they'll probably say this thing from The List to you: "Do as I say, not as I do."

Most people are trying to do the best they can, but nobody does the best all the time. It's just a whole lot easier to *know* the right thing to do all the time than to *do* the right thing all the time. Maybe somebody will try to teach you that smoking cigarettes is bad for your health, and then you catch them smoking. Maybe somebody will try to teach you to be honest, and then you catch them cheating. It could happen lots of different ways, but someday you're going to see someone you learn from doing something they told you was bad to do.

"Do as I say, not as I do" is not just a way to teach you that nobody's perfect. The big meaning of "Do as I say, not as I do," is this: *The right thing is bigger than any teacher.* The right thing to do is right, and the good thing to do is good, even if the people you love or the people who teach you don't do it. The right thing is kind of like a ruler. It's the way we measure how good we are. Even when we don't measure up, the ruler that measures good and bad, right and wrong, is still there. Everybody gets measured, because the right thing is more important than anyone, even more important than the people you love.

All this may be a hard thing for you to learn if you're like most kids and grow up thinking that your mom and your dad are perfect. If you just remember that they were people before they were parents, you'll have an easier time of it. And after you understand that your parents are not perfect, you can see much more clearly all the things about them that *are* perfect.

If you want perfect, go to God. But if you want somebody to tuck you in at night and somebody to love you as much as they can and as deeply as they can, then you need people. People aren't perfect, but people are real and close and warm, and that's just about as close to perfect as we get down here on planet Earth.

BECAUSE I SAY SO

I bet I know the thing on The List that makes you the most angry. You want to do something, and your folks tell you that you can't, and you ask, *"Why?"* and they give you some reason, and then you ask again, *"Whyyyy?"* and they give you some other reason, and you say, *"But whyyyyyyyyy?"* And then they hit you with something that drives you wild. They say, "All right! You want a reason. Here's the reason.... Because I say so!"

And then you go ballistic and maybe, on your way out of the house or up to your room, you will make sure they hear you say, "That's no reason! You are *so* unfair!" And then they will go back to doing what they were doing, or maybe they will let you know as you leave, "Get used to it. Life's not fair." Or maybe they will use this version, "When you have your own home, you can do whatever you want, but as long as you live here, you have to do what I say."

What I'm about to do may seem impossible, but I'm going to try it anyway. I'm going to try to explain to you why "Because I say so" is a good reason for doing something, and why you shouldn't get angry when you hear it, and why it will definitely be one of the first things you will say to your kids when you grow up.

There are reasons for everything. The hard part in life is learning how to tell the difference between a good reason and a bad reason. When your folks tell you not to touch the burners on the stove, and you ask why, and they say, "Because the burners are hot and you'll hurt yourself if you touch them," it's easy to know that you just heard a good reason. When somebody you know tells you, "Go ahead—take this drug; everybody else is doing it and you don't want to be left out," it should also be easy for you to know that you just heard a bad reason.

The problem with life is that it is not always so easy to know if you just heard a good reason or a bad reason for doing something. Sometimes people who give you good reasons don't speak that well or don't look cool, but they're still giving you good reasons. And sometimes people who give you bad reasons are slick and beautiful, but their reasons are still bad.

One of the best ways to tell if you are getting a good reason is to ask yourself, "Do I trust this person who is giving me this reason?" If you trust somebody, it means that the person has shown you in the past that he or she cares about you and wants to help you and would not do anything to hurt you. So if somebody you trust gives you a reason, it probably is a good one. Now, even people you trust can let you down or give you bad reasons, but people you don't trust will give you bad reasons almost all the time.

Sometimes the people you trust can't give you the whole reason for doing something or for not doing something. Sometimes the whole reason is too long or too complicated. Sometimes the whole reason has secret stuff in it that you are not supposed to know. Sometimes the whole reason might scare you. This is when the person giving you the reason might say, "Do it [or don't do it] because I say so." What they are really saying to you is, "Trust me. I love you and I would never ask you to do anything bad. Do this [or don't do this] because of that love and trust, and everything will be all right."

So that's the big meaning behind "Because I say so": *You have to love and trust good people if you are going to grow up good.*

Now, there is just one problem. Loving and trusting people who do real bad things, even if they are

your parents, is a bad idea. But when you find somebody who lives a good life, somebody who is always
trying to do the right thing for you and for other
people, somebody who loves and trusts you—well,
you should love and trust that person right back and
hang on to him or her for the rest of your life. And
when that good person says to you, "Because I say
so," you should say to yourself and to them, "That's
a good enough reason for me."

ITS TIME FOR BED

In your life there is a time for everything.

There's a time to be born and a time to die, a time to plant and a time to pick what you planted, a time to cry and a time to laugh. There's a time to build a swing set and a time to tear down that swing set and build something new, a time to buy stuff and a time to save so that you can buy stuff later. There's a time to stay in your room because you are mad at the whole wide world and a time to go out to a party and dance and shout and sing. There's a big time to read books and a little time to watch television, a time to play games that make you run and a time to play games that make you think, a time to sit still and a time to jump around like a crazy animal.

There's a time to get something you love and a time to lose something you love. There's a time to be sad because somebody you loved a lot just died and a time to be happy because you know that God is taking care of that person's soul for ever and ever. There's a time to be young and a time to be old. There's a time to stay up and there is a...TIME FOR BED!

Learning about life is mostly learning what time it is.

To know what time it is for you, to know what's all right for you to do now and what is not all right for you to do now takes something called *discipline*. Discipline is being able to stop yourself from doing something you really want to do because you know it isn't the right time. And discipline also means doing something you don't want to do because you know it *is* the right time.

So when you get told "It's time for bed," mostly it's about you getting enough sleep so that you won't fall asleep in class tomorrow, but it's also about teaching you this: *You need to learn discipline.* Discipline is like an alarm clock deep inside of you that goes off when it's the right time for you to do or not do something.

All people who do great things have discipline. They've learned the right times to do things. They've learned how to give up what they want to do now so that they can do what they *really* want to do later. They understand that just wanting to do something doesn't make it the right time to do that thing. The people who do really well in life are usually the people who don't go to bed when they want to; they go to bed when it's time.

But don't think that if you have discipline you have to say no to everything good. Discipline is also a way of teaching you how to say yes to other good things. Saying no to television means saying yes to books. Saying no to goofing off means saying yes to learning. Saying no to staying up late means saying yes to sleep and yes to dreams about all the things you can do when you wake up and it's the right time!

SAY YOUR PRAYERS

How do you get ready for bed?

Do you wash your face and then put on your pajamas, or do you just dive into bed? Do you brush your teeth up and down for a few minutes, or do you just brush for a few seconds until the toothpaste gets foamy and then spit it out? Do you arrange your stuffed animals around your bed and close the closet door to protect you against the boogie monsters, or do you get your dog to sleep near your bed? No matter what you do when you get ready for bed, you should never forget to say your prayers. That's the big reason "Say your prayers" is on The List: *You need to find some time in your day to check in with God.*

Checking in with God is easy *and* hard. The hard part is that you can't see God. The easy part is that God is always listening. God is always near to you, and God is always rooting for you, and God is always betting that you will turn out great!

Now, you might be one of the kids who doesn't believe in God. That's okay. You have lots of time to find God in your life. If you do believe in God, the time when you're in bed but not yet asleep is a great time to check in with God. It's a great time to pray. You're quiet, and you're not moving around. You have time to think about what happened during the day, how you messed up and how you did good. You have time to think about the people you love and to send healing thoughts to the sick people you love. It's a good time for thinking and a great time for praying.

There are really only four kinds of prayers: thanks, gimme, oops, and wow. It would be great if you found time every night to pray each kind of prayer.

Thanks prayers thank God for giving you the things you can't buy, things like love and health, laughs and smiles, families and friends. When you thank God for all these great things you have, the things you don't have won't matter that much anymore.

Gimme prayers are the kind of prayers in which you ask God to give you something. Asking God for a new bike or stereo is silly, because God doesn't run a store, and you can work and save for those things.

But if you are praying to God to make your grandma well or to make your dad not so angry, those are great gimme prayers, because some things only God can give you.

Oops prayers are the ones you say when you mess up. Everybody messes up, because nobody is perfect. The big thing about messing up is figuring out how to make things right. Oops prayers help with that. By telling God what you did wrong, you are also telling yourself, and when you do that you can get confidence and courage to go out there and try to make things right again.

Wow prayers are the ones you say when you are wowed by something you saw in the world that day. Maybe the wow thing you saw that day was a beautiful sunset, or maybe it was a big wave or a cute puppy or a nest of birds. The world is so beautiful, there is just no good reason for you to go through even one day without saying wow. And if you say wow to yourself, you should really say wow to God, who is the maker of every wow you will ever see or feel or hear.

Just remember that even if you need practice talking to God, God does not need any practice listening to you. Listening to your thanks, gimme, oops, and wow prayers is one of God's most favorite things to do!

I LOVE YOU

Not everything your folks tell you all the time is annoying. Lots of things they tell you all the time are nice and sweet and warm and fuzzy, and the best of all is just three short words: "I love you."

It's pretty simple. Kids who hear "I love you" usually turn out all right, and kids who don't, often don't. You need people in your life who care for you more than they care for themselves, who want things for you that they deny themselves, and who pray for you even when you are not praying for yourself.

You may wonder why your folks are always telling you they love you. You know they love you, and they know you know that they love you. So why is it so important to say "I love you" all the time? The reason is the same reason that you need to smile. The world has such great funny and wonderful things in it that no matter how hard you try not to smile, smiles are just going to happen whenever you bump into something great, funny, or wonderful in the world.

It's just the same with saying "I love you." There is always something new about the person you love that you're seeing right then for the first time. There is always some moment when you're so full of love that it just spills out of you. Sometimes it spills out into hugs and sometimes into kisses and sometimes it spills out into the words "I love you." If you really love somebody, you can't say "I love you" too many times.

"I love you" is the reason for The List. "I love you" is the reason people care about how you're growing up and how you're acting toward other people. "I love you" is the reason they nag you to wear clean underwear, eat your vegetables, take out the garbage, look both ways before you cross the street, keep your shoes off the couch, share your toys, tie your shoes, walk the dog, say please and thank you, clean your plate, do your homework, cover your mouth when you sneeze, stand up straight, say you're sorry, go give Grandma a kiss, call if you're going to be late, and say your prayers. It's the reason they say you shouldn't pee in the pool, talk with your mouth full, talk to your father/mother like that, judge a book by its cover, or hit people. It's why you hear them say over and over, "Do as I say, not as I do" and "Money doesn't grow on trees, you know" and "It's time for bed" and "I hope that when you grow up, you'll have a kid just like you" and "Because I say so" and a whole lot of other stuff that will go on The List someday.

So go to your mom and dad right now, or call them on the phone, or say a prayer to God in heaven who is taking care of their souls, and say something like this (These are my words to my dad, Sol Gellman, and mom, Rosalie Gellman. You can use them, but your own words will be much better):

Dear Mom and Dad,

I love you, and I wanted to say it to you right here and right now because you said it so often to me. You said "I love you" so many ways. You said it with The List, and you said it with your lives.

I have always tried to say "I love you" to Mara and Max just the way you said it to me. I hope I can say "I love you" to the children of Mara and Max someday, but even if I can't, I will feel it in my heart, and they will know it. And something in their voice when they say "I love you" to their children will come from my voice and my soul.

Because of all the "I love you's" you said to me when I was growing up, I have always believed that everything will be all right. Because of your "I love you's" I know that after God kisses me and takes my breath away, the first words I will hear after I die will come from God, telling me in a sweet and forever voice, "I love you." And I also know that the first words I am going to say to God with all my heart and with all my soul and with all my might are these words:

"I love you, too."